dear DRAGON

written by
Josh Funk

illustrated by
Rodolfo Montalvo

Viking

Hello, students!

Our poetry and pen pal projects
this year are combined.

Upon your desks you'll see the pen pals
that you've been assigned.

Please make sure the letters that you write are all in rhyme.

Now open up your envelopes because it's pen pal time!

September 12th

Dear Blaise Dragomir,

We haven't met each other, and
I don't know what to say.

I really don't like writing,
but I'll do it anyway.

Yesterday my dad and I
designed a giant fort.

I like playing catch and soccer.
What's your favorite sport?

Sincerely,
George Slair

October 1st

Dear George Slair,

I also don't like writing, but
I'll try it, I suppose.

A fort is like a castle, right?
I love attacking those.

My favorite sport is skydiving.
I jump near Falcor Peak.

Tomorrow is my birthday but
my party is next week.

Sincerely,
Blaise Dragomir

October 31st

Dear Blaise Dragomir,

You know how to skydive? That's as awesome as it gets!

My dog destroyed my fort last night. Do you have any pets?

Happy birthday, by the way! I don't have mine till June.

I'm trick-or-treating as a knight. We're heading out real soon.

George Slair

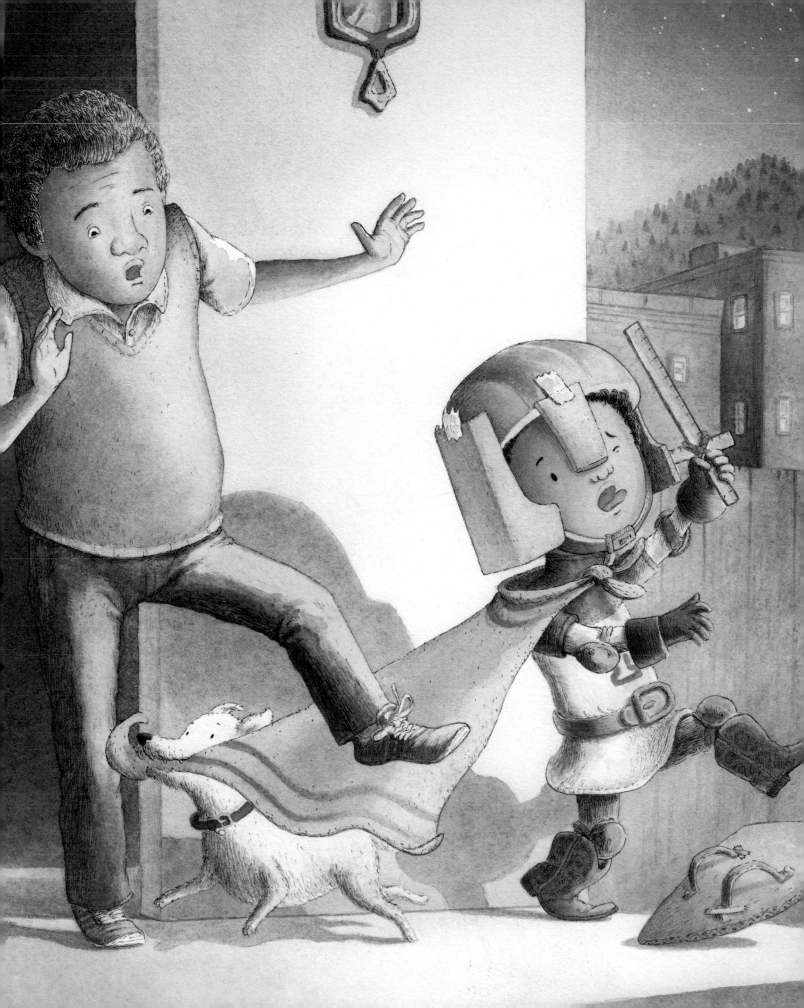

November 14th

Dear George Slair,

Knights are super-scary! I
don't like to trick-or-treat.

Brushing teeth is such a pain,
I rarely eat a sweet.

My pet's a Bengal kitten and
tonight she needs a bath.

What's your favorite class in
school? I'm really into math!

Blaise Dragomir

December 16th

Dear Blaise D.,

My favorite class is art. I made a mold of my left hand.

Next we'll craft mosaics using pebbles, stones, and sand.

Yesterday I won a prize in this year's science fair.

My towering volcano blasted lava everywhere!

George S.

January 18th

Dear George S.,

My father's won our local fire-breathing contest twice.

He still retains the record, melting fifty cubes of ice.

Do you have any hobbies? I enjoy collecting rocks.

I keep them in a secret place inside a precious box.

Blaise D.

February 22nd

Blaise,

Fire breathing? What's your father's job? My folks are teachers.

I collect exotic monsters, animals, and creatures.

Oh, guess what! I heard the news this morning from Miss Sweet.

A pen pal picnic's planned for June! At last we'll get to meet!

George

March 15th

George,

Dad's in demolition. He works
   hard throughout the day.

But every night we read a book
   or pick a game to play.

Soon he's gonna take me flying,
   once it's really spring.

It's such a rush to ride the air
   that flows from wing to wing.

Blaise

April 11th

Hi, Blaise!

Skydiving <u>and</u> flying lessons? Wow, your parents rock!

I'm lucky if my father lets me bike around the block.

Once the school year's over and this project is complete,

should we continue writing? 'Cause it could be kind of neat. . . .

Your friend, George

May 12th

Hey, George!

I'm psyched about the picnic and
  I can't wait to attend.

Who'd have thought this pen pal
  thing would make me a new friend?

Writing more sounds awesome.
  I was gonna ask you, too!

I've never liked to write as much
  as when I write to you.

Your friend, Blaise

"Blaise?"

"George?"

"My pen pal is a dragon?"

"My pen pal is a human?"

"Our plan was a success, my friend,
or so it would appear!"

"The Poetry and Pen Pal Project!
Once again next year?"

Dear Lauren, thank you for encouraging me, supporting me, and continuing to put up with my shenanigans. —J.F.

To my dear little nieces Lilyana and Azelie. —R.M.

VIKING
Penguin Young Readers Group
An imprint of Penguin Random House LLC
375 Hudson Street
New York, New York 10014

First published in the United States of America by Viking,
an imprint of Penguin Random House LLC, 2016

Text copyright © 2016 by Josh Funk
Illustrations copyright © 2016 by Rodolfo Montalvo

LIBRARY OF CONGRESS CATALOGING-IN-PUBLICATION DATA IS AVAILABLE
ISBN: 978-0-451-47230-4

Manufactured in China   Designed by Kate Renner

5   7   9   10   8   6

The artwork for this book was created with watercolors, black acrylic ink, and graphite.